Itty ♔ Bitty PRINCESS Kitty

3

The Cloud Race

by Melody Mews   illustrated by Ellen Stubbings

LITTLE SIMON
New York   London   Toronto   Sydney   New Delhi

This book is a work of fiction. Any references to historical events, real people, or real places are used fictitiously. Other names, characters, places, and events are products of the author's imagination, and any resemblance to actual events or places or persons, living or dead, is entirely coincidental.

LITTLE SIMON

An imprint of Simon & Schuster Children's Publishing Division
1230 Avenue of the Americas, New York, New York 10020
First Little Simon hardcover edition October 2020. Copyright © 2020 by Simon & Schuster,
Inc. All rights reserved, including the right of reproduction in whole or in part in any form.
LITTLE SIMON is a registered trademark of Simon & Schuster, Inc., and associated colophon is a
trademark of Simon & Schuster, Inc. For information about special discounts for bulk purchases,
please contact Simon & Schuster Special Sales at 1-866-506-1949
or business@simonandschuster.com.
The Simon & Schuster Speakers Bureau can bring authors to your live event. For more
information or to book an event contact the Simon & Schuster Speakers Bureau at
1-866-248-3049 or visit our website at www.simonspeakers.com.
Designed by Laura Roode. The text of this book was set in Banda.
Manufactured in the United States of America 0820 FFG
2 4 6 8 10 9 7 5 3 1
Cataloging-in-Publication Data is available for this title from the Library of Congress.
ISBN 978-1-5344-6641-8 (hc)
ISBN 978-1-5344-6640-1 (pbk)
ISBN 978-1-5344-6642-5 (eBook)

Contents

Chapter 1   News at Mermaid Cove   1

Chapter 2   Never Annoy an Announcement Fairy   11

Chapter 3   The Queen's Advice   23

Chapter 4   The Rules of Racing   33

Chapter 5   Itty in the Driver's Seat   45

Chapter 6   Rules Are Rules   57

Chapter 7   The Big Day   71

Chapter 8   Ready, Set, Race!   81

Chapter 9   A Helping Hand . . . or Paw   95

Chapter 10   And the Winner Is . . .   107

News at
Mermaid Cove

Itty Bitty Princess Kitty, Luna Unicorn, Esme Butterfly, and Chipper Bunny were hanging out at one of their favorite spots in Lollyland: Mermaid Cove.

"I hope we see a mermaid today," Itty said. "I love hearing them sing."

"Me too," Esme agreed. "That's why this is the *best* place in Lollyland."

"What about Goodie Grove?" Chipper asked.

Goodie Grove was a hop, skip, and a jump from Mermaid Cove, and it was *the* place to go for delicious treats.

"I don't think I could pick one favorite place," Itty said. "What about you, Luna?"

"Hmmmm . . ." Luna looked thoughtful. "Maybe it's someplace we haven't been yet, like Hot Chocolate Springs. My sister, Stella, went there with her class last week!" A little bit of glitter spurted from Luna's horn, which always happened when she was excited. "I wish we could go!"

"Itty, since your dad is King of Lollyland, can you ask him to change the rule that says you have to be ten years old to visit the springs?" Chipper asked.

"I've tried!" Itty sighed. "But

he said the rule is there for a reason. Something about being big enough to float on the marshmallows."

Suddenly there was a ripple in the water. Itty and her friends forgot all about Hot Chocolate Springs as a shimmering mermaid emerged and began to sing.

"You may not be old enough
for Hot Chocolate Springs,
But you are old enough for
some wonderful things.
It is almost time for the
Lollyland Cloud Race,
An event so fun it will bring
a smile to your face!"

Itty and her friends applauded as the mermaid dove back under the water.

The Cloud Race! Itty had totally forgotten about the annual event.

"Do you know what this means?" she asked her friends.

"That we're finally old enough to enter the Cloud Race!" Luna cheered. "And our announcement fairies should be arriving soon."

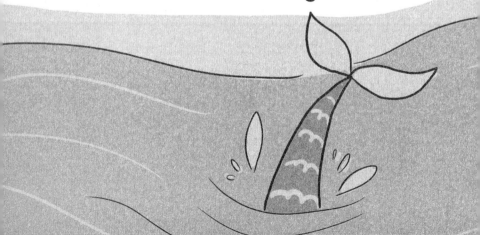

chapter 2

Never Annoy an Announcement Fairy

There were many types of fairies in Lollyland, and they all had very important jobs. Sugar fairies collected syrup from the river, construction fairies built houses, and announcement fairies made special announcements, to name just a few.

"I wonder when all our announcement fairies will come," Luna said as the friends walked home.

"I see one," Esme whispered.

Everyone froze. Fairies could be a little bit fussy, and announcement fairies especially disliked shouting. They also didn't like delivering messages in front of a crowd.

The fairy flitted around, finally landing on a branch near Chipper.

With her back to the girls, she faced Chipper and blew into her miniature trumpet.

Itty tried to listen to the announcement, but she only caught the end of it when the fairy asked Chipper what his answer was.

"I'm in!" Chipper yelled.

"There's no need to shout!"
The fairy stomped her feet and
flew away.

Itty and her friends waited
until the fairy was far enough
away before bursting into excited
giggles. Then they decided to go
home separately so they could
each be alone when their fairy
arrived.

Itty was in a field near the palace when her fairy landed on a tall flower. She took out her trumpet and began to blow into it.

"I know why you're here!" Itty exclaimed. Then she clapped a hand over her mouth.

The fairy was scowling, clearly not happy that Itty had ruined her announcement.

"Sorry!" Itty cried. "I'm just so excited about the race. And I definitely want to enter."

"Fine," the fairy squeaked before flying off in a huff.

Itty breathed a sigh of relief.

"Princess Itty, the Cloud Race can be dangerous!"

Itty looked around to see who was speaking. It was a flower! The flowers of Lollyland didn't speak often, but when they did it was wise to listen.

"Dangerous?" Itty repeated.

Uh-oh. Had she missed some sort of warning when she interrupted the fairy?

The Queen's Advice

Itty ran inside to find her parents. She had to learn more about the Cloud Race.

"Mom! Dad! Guess what?" Itty shouted as she ran through the entrance hall.

"Darling, don't run indoors,"

Itty's mom reminded her. "And please don't shout. An announcement fairy just left, and you know how they dislike shouting."

"An announcement fairy was here?" Itty asked.

"Yes, she came to tell us that the invitations for the Cloud Race had all been delivered," the King replied. His eyes twinkled as he smiled at Itty. "We understand you've already accepted yours."

"About that," Itty began. "I kind of interrupted the fairy and she got mad and wouldn't finish her announcement, so I accepted without hearing everything. . . ." Itty paused and looked at her parents' faces. They were still smiling, which meant they weren't upset. Yet.

"But then a flower told me that the races can be . . . *dangerous*. Is that true?"

"Well, they can be," the Queen said, placing a hand on Itty's shoulder. "But there's nothing to

worry about. All of the racers now participate in a week of training to learn how to safely steer their clouds."

"Phew!" Itty exclaimed. "So the race is totally safe?"

"Well, yes." The king scratched his chin. "As long as you follow the rules."

"What does that mean?" Itty asked.

"It means you probably don't want to hear about the year your mom veered off course and landed in the Syrup River," Itty's dad replied, chuckling at the memory.

"Well, at least I didn't collide with a sloth!" the Queen replied. "Or was it two sloths?"

Veering off course? Collisions with sloths? What had Itty gotten herself into?

Noticing her worried expression, Itty's mom squeezed her shoulder.

"Just pay attention during your lessons and you'll be fine."

♥ chapter 4 ♥

The Rules of Racing

After school the next day, Itty and her friends headed to a special meeting for all the racers at Cloud Park. A circle of log seats was set up next to the rows of parked clouds. Itty, Luna, Esme, and Chipper found seats as a dapper peacock walked

into the center of the circle. He gave a loud whistle and everyone quieted down.

"Fine listening skills!" he said as he strutted around the circle.

"Those will come in handy during your lessons. But first, I am Mr. Feathers, Grand Master of the Cloud Race."

Mr. Feathers paused dramatically. Itty looked around, unsure of what to do. Luna started clapping, so Itty did too. Soon everyone was clapping. Mr. Feathers smiled, bowed, and continued talking.

Just then, a fox took a seat next to Itty. She recognized him as being in Stella's class. His name was Wily.

"What'd I miss?" Wily asked.

Itty didn't respond, since Mr. Feathers was talking.

"I said, what'd I miss?" Wily repeated in a louder voice.

"There are three very important rules you must remember," Mr. Feathers was saying. "The first rule is to keep your arms, legs, wings, beaks, horns, and so on *inside* the cloud at all times. The next rule is to always pass on the right. The third and final rule is perhaps the most important one. . . ."

Itty scooted forward in her seat to make sure she could hear clearly.

"You must remember to slow down before going around a curve. Otherwise you risk getting thrown off your cloud. We don't want that, do we?"

"No," Itty murmured along with the other animals.

"Rules shmools!" Itty heard Wily say to the porcupine next to him.

"I don't need any rules," he continued. "And you know what else I don't need? Driving lessons!" He and the porcupine high-fived.

Itty in the
Driver's Seat

Unlike Wily Fox, Itty was glad to have driving lessons. She had ridden on clouds many times, but *riding* was different than *driving*. Itty was both nervous and excited.

On the first day of lessons, the racers learned how to get into

the driver's seat. Itty was used to
sitting in back as a passenger, but
drivers had to sit up front. It was
a little scary at first, but Itty got
used to it and discovered she loved
being in control of her cloud.

The next day, the racers learned steering. Clouds didn't have steering wheels, so you patted the cloud on the same side as the direction you wanted to move. Itty learned that she was really good at this. Mr. Feathers even complimented her gentle patting style.

On the third day, the students learned how to make the clouds go faster by tapping their right foot, or slower by tapping their left foot. This was the thing that made Itty the most nervous. She didn't

want to accidentally go too fast and get thrown from her cloud! But after lots of practice, she found it was pretty easy to use the correct foot to speed up or slow down. Mr. Feathers repeated the

rule about always remembering
to slow down around curves.

Finally, after several days of
lessons, it was time for the trial
races. The animals were divided
into smaller groups. Itty was in
the blue group, Luna and Chipper

were in the orange group, and Esme was in the red group. Itty recognized a few kids from school in her group, including Wily Fox.

Itty climbed onto her cloud and settled into the driver's seat. She had just started moving when Wily zipped past her.

As Itty carefully made her way around the track, Wily passed her again. But Itty kept going slow and steady. After all, today was about practicing, not winning. Itty had plenty of time to worry about that later—after she was an expert driver.

Rules Are Rules

By the final day of practice, Itty felt good about her driving skills. She hadn't won any of the blue group's practice races, but she'd finished second twice.

Itty joined the other racers as Mr. Feathers strutted to the

center of the circle. The kids immediately began to clap—they had figured out by now that Mr. Feathers loved applause.

"My dear students." Mr. Feathers smiled and bowed. "Congratulations on completing your training! You now have three days to practice on your own before the official race. Just remember the rules as you're practicing and we'll all have a safe and exciting race. I'll see you on the big day!"

As the animals left the circle,

Itty said goodbye to her new friends from the blue group. She was looking for Luna, Esme, and Chipper when she heard Wily's voice. She couldn't see who he was talking to, but she could hear what he was saying. It was something about adding boosters to his cloud to make it go faster during the race.

Itty turned around. Whoever Wily had been talking to was gone. Itty knew she had to say something, so she cleared her throat and took a deep breath. "I

heard what you said about adding
boosters to your cloud. That's
not right, Wily," Itty said firmly.
"That's cheating."

Wily didn't seem to care that Itty had overheard him. "Mr. Feathers never said we couldn't modify our clouds. You race your way and I'll race mine," he told her. Then he walked away.

Itty bit her lip. It was true that Mr. Feathers hadn't specifically said they couldn't use boosters, but she was pretty sure it was against the rules. Should she tell Mr. Feathers?

Just then, Esme, Luna, and Chipper came running over.

"Itty! Luna won all three of our practice races today!" Chipper shouted.

"Wow, Luna, that's so great!" Itty cried.

Laughing and celebrating with her friends on their way home, Itty forgot all about Wily and the cloud boosters.

The Big Day

Over the next three days, Itty had a great time practicing with her friends. It was easy to see how Luna had won three practice races—she was a *really* good driver!

Finally, it was the day of the big race. Itty, Luna, Chipper, and Esme met up at the palace and headed over to Cloud Park together.

"Luna, I think you have a really good chance of winning the race," Itty said.

Esme and Chipper agreed.

"I don't know about that." Luna smiled bashfully. "There are a lot of great racers, including all of you. I'm just excited to be in the race, whether I win or not."

When they reached Cloud Park, Itty hugged her friends and wished them luck. The racers were instructed to line up at the starting gate with the drivers from

their practice groups. Itty spotted
the blue group and made her way
over to them.

As she settled onto her cloud,
Itty could feel the excitement

in the air. She looked up to the stands. They were really crowded, but Itty was pretty sure she spotted her dad's royal robe and saw her mom waving.

Two clouds over from Itty, she noticed Wily in a shiny yellow racing jacket. She tried to get a better look at his cloud. Were there boosters on it? But she realized

she didn't know what boosters looked like, or even where to look for them. There was no way for her to tell if Wily had added them.

Just then, Mr. Feathers appeared.
He was holding the special green
flag that signaled the race was
about to begin!

chapter 8

Ready, Set, Race!

"On your mark, get set . . . GO!"

The moment the green flag was raised, Itty and the other racers took off. Several clouds zipped past her, but Itty slowly built up speed as she moved higher and higher to the top track of the course. There were three tracks, and racers could choose the level they wanted to fly the course on. Itty liked the top track because it allowed her to see what was happening below her.

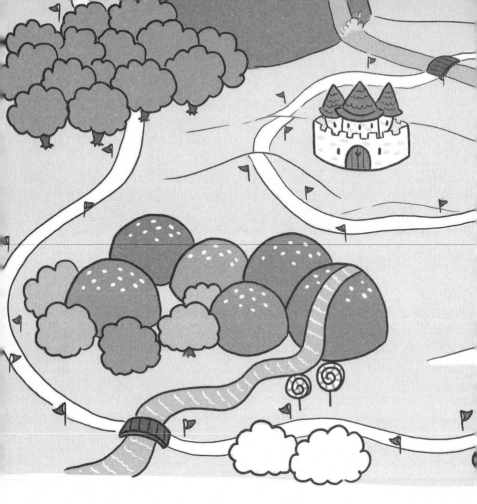

Plus, the track went all over Lollyland, so it was like taking a tour of the kingdom. Itty loved getting a

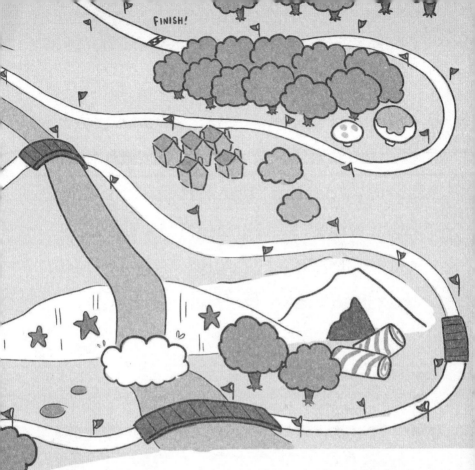

cloud's-eye view of Goodie Grove,
Starfish Falls, and Mermaid Cove,
and she even spotted some places
she hadn't yet explored.

Itty began to pick up speed, catching up with the cloud in front of her. She took a deep breath and gently patted her cloud on the right side. It worked! Itty's cloud glided safely around the cloud that had been in front of her.

On the track below, Itty spotted
Luna just ahead of her. It looked
like Luna was in the lead. She
tried to spot Esme and Chipper
but couldn't find them.

In the distance, Itty could see that a sharp curve was coming up, so she started to slow down. Most of the racers around her did the same, but one cloud zipped by

her superfast. Itty tried not to let this distract her and focused on maintaining the perfect speed— fast enough to stay in the race, but slow enough to take the curve safely.

CAUTION!
SLOW

ZOOM!

As Itty approached the curve, she heard yelling. From the corner of her eye, she could see someone flying through the air . . . and off the track! She recognized the yellow racing jacket and realized it was Wily.

He had taken the curve too fast
and gotten thrown off course!

A Helping
Hand . . . or Paw

As she went around the curve, Itty
could see Wily off to her right. He
and his cloud were tangled up in
the branches of a tree.

Itty kept going, having picked
up momentum after the curve.
She was sure someone would go

help Wily. But what if no one did? What if no one else had seen what happened? If Itty turned around now, she knew she would give up her chance of winning the race. But she also knew that if Wily was truly stuck, she had to help him.

As she steered her cloud to turn around, other racers whipped past her. Most of them gave her confused looks but kept going.

Itty flew back and parked her cloud next to Wily's, careful not to get herself tangled in the branches. "You look like you could use help," she said to Wily.

Wily didn't say anything, but Itty saw him nod. She reached over and gently patted Wily's cloud to let it know it had to move up and over to get free from the branches. It took a few moments, but soon Wily and his cloud were untangled.

"Are you okay?" Itty asked.

Wily nodded again.

"What happened? Was it . . . the boosters? Did they make you speed up by mistake?"

Wily finally looked up. He looked embarrassed. "No, I didn't use boosters. I thought about it, and I knew you were right that using them would be cheating."

Itty didn't understand. "So you accidentally went around the curve too fast?"

Now Wily looked even more embarrassed. "No, it wasn't an accident. I know Mr. Feathers said to slow down when going around a curve, but I just really wanted to win. So I sped up instead."

Itty nodded. "Well, I'm glad you didn't get hurt."

"It was really nice of you to stop and help me," Wily said. "But now you've ruined your chance of winning the race."

Itty shrugged. "I think I need a little more practice, anyway. There's always next year!"

As Itty and Wily made their way back to the track, they heard cheering in the distance.

The race was over! But who had won?

And the Winner Is . . .

"Well, should we finish the race?" Itty asked Wily.

Wily grinned. "Let's do it!"

Itty and Wily sped off together. Wily was racing much more carefully now. He slowed down for the next curve. He and Itty were

neck and neck as they approached
the finish line.

As she crossed the finish line,

Itty saw glitter everywhere.

All that glitter could only mean

one thing. . . .

"Luna, did you win?!" Itty cried as she spotted her best friend in the winner's circle.

Luna ran over and pulled Itty in for a hug.

"Yes!" Luna exclaimed. "Can you believe it?"

"Of course I can." Itty laughed as bits of glitter landed on her nose. "You practiced so hard and you're a natural. I'm so happy for you!"

"Congratulations, Luna," Wily added.

Just then, Mr. Feathers came over and placed a wing around Luna's shoulders. "It's time for the awards ceremony," he said,

steering Luna toward the stage, where a group of art fairies dressed in berets and smocks stood. They were holding something covered with a silky tarp.

One of the fairies pulled the tarp off to reveal Luna's prize—a beautiful, glittering miniature sculpture of a unicorn that looked just like Luna racing on a fluffy cloud.

"Wow, the art fairies whipped that up quickly," Itty murmured. She watched happily as Luna's fans surrounded her.

"Thanks again for helping me," Wily said shyly. "Next time, I'll follow all the rules!"

Itty smiled. "Well, I don't think this is a rule, but I do think we're supposed to be celebrating right now," she said.

And together, she and Wily joined Luna, Chipper, Esme, and the rest of the racers in a big Cloud Race celebration.

Here's a sneak
peek at Itty's next
royal adventure!

It was dinnertime in Lollyland, and Itty Bitty Princess Kitty was hiding in one of her favorite places in the palace—the royal kitchen!

"Peaches, are you adding *marshmallows*?" Itty whispered.

Itty wasn't supposed to be there, but Peaches was a very friendly fairy. The other fairies weren't mean, but they didn't like to be bothered, especially Garbanzo, the head food fairy.

Peaches looked over at Garbanzo, who was making a soufflé. There were tiny spice bottles all over the counter.

"Yes, it's a *fairy* secret," Peaches squeaked. She flew over and gave Itty a fairy-size mug. "Here, have a taste!"

Itty sipped the soup. "It's so tasty!" she exclaimed.

"Does it need more?" Peaches asked.

"Nope!" Itty assured her. "It's perfect."

Peaches happily flew back to the pot. Then as she struggled to pick up a giant spoon, another fairy rushed over.